FRANCE RAPE TRIAL OF DOMINIQUE PELICOT

GISÈLE PELICOT'S EX-HUSBAND FOUND GUILTY IN MASS RAPE TRIAL

ALEXIS I. THOMPSON

Table of Contents

Introduction

In the heart of France, where cobblestone streets meander through picturesque villages and family gatherings echo with laughter, a chilling story unfolded—one that would shatter illusions and ignite a national reckoning. At the center of it stood Gisèle Pelicot, a 72-year-old grandmother, whose life of quiet contentment masked a horror so profound it would galvanize a country.

For nearly a decade, Gisèle's husband, Dominique Pelicot, betrayed her in unimaginable ways. In the privacy of their retirement home in Mazan, Dominique orchestrated a series of atrocities: drugging his wife, assaulting her, and inviting dozens of strangers to do the same while she lay unconscious. More than 20,000 photos and videos meticulously cataloged these crimes, hidden behind the façade of a devoted husband and grandfather.

When the truth emerged, the world recoiled in disbelief. How could such monstrosity exist in plain sight? Yet from the depths of this tragedy rose an unlikely hero. Gisèle, once a private and unassuming woman, made a bold decision: to strip away her anonymity, confront her abusers in open court, and become a beacon of hope for survivors everywhere.

Chapter 1

The Perfect Life

At first glance, Gisèle and Dominique Pelicot's life seemed like a storybook romance. Childhood sweethearts, they had met at 19 and spent the next 50 years building a life together. They raised three children and retired to the charming town of Mazan in Provence, a haven where they hosted their grandchildren for summers filled with laughter and sunshine. Dominique was known for his long bike rides, while Gisèle loved exploring the local countryside on foot. To their neighbors, they were the epitome of a happy, fulfilled couple entering their golden years.

But behind the façade of harmony, cracks began to form. Gisèle suffered from mysterious health problems: dramatic weight loss, unexplained hair thinning, and frequent blackouts. Doctors offered no concrete answers, leaving her to endure the discomfort while relying on Dominique's attentive care. He was the devoted husband, driving her to appointments, monitoring her medications, and reassuring their children that everything was under control.

The truth, however, was far darker than anyone could have imagined. Beneath his veneer of compassion, Dominique harbored a monstrous secret. Gisèle's symptoms were not a medical anomaly but the result of his calculated and sinister acts. Every meal he prepared, every drink he handed her, was laced with tranquilizers designed to render her unconscious. It was a deception so elaborate and cruel that even those closest to them remained oblivious.

In the quiet town of Mazan, Gisèle lived unknowingly at the center of a nightmare—a nightmare that would soon unravel and expose unimaginable betrayal.

Chapter 2

The Revelation

The illusion shattered on a quiet September day in 2020. Dominique Pelicot's meticulously hidden double life began to unravel not at home, but in the mundane setting of a supermarket. Caught filming up the skirts of unsuspecting women, Dominique's secret compulsions were exposed. Security guards detained him, and the police seized his phone, uncovering the first clues to the horrors concealed within his seemingly ordinary existence.

The officers' initial discovery of illicit photos and videos was enough to prompt further investigation. They obtained a warrant to search the Pelicot home, where they uncovered a trove of digital evidence. Among the 20,000 meticulously organized photos and videos were recordings of Gisèle, unconscious and being assaulted. The evidence painted a damning picture: a husband drugging his wife and inviting strangers to abuse her, all while documenting the crimes for his own gratification.

Gisèle was in Paris with her grandchildren when Dominique broke the news of his supermarket arrest. Tearful and apologetic, he framed the incident as a one-time lapse in judgment. Ever loyal, Gisèle forgave him, chalking it up to a fleeting moral failing. She had no idea that this confession was merely the tip of the iceberg.

Two months later, the police summoned her to the station. What followed was a revelation so devastating it defied comprehension: her loving husband had been her greatest betrayer. Confronted with the grotesque truth, Gisèle's world crumbled, leaving her with an agonizing choice—retreat into silence or fight back against the unthinkable.

Chapter 3

A Shattered World

For Gisèle Pelicot, the revelations from the police were incomprehensible. Sitting in the sterile confines of the station, she listened as officers detailed the horrors buried in her husband's digital archives. Images and videos—tens of thousands of them—documented years of abuse she had unknowingly endured. The man she had trusted for decades, the father of her children, had systematically drugged her, assaulted her, and invited strangers to do the same.

The betrayal was a cruel paradox. Dominique had been her closest confidant, the person she leaned on for comfort during her unexplained blackouts and deteriorating health. Now she learned that the very symptoms she had suffered were caused by his hand. Every meal, every drink he had prepared, had been laced with tranquilizers, stripping her of consciousness and autonomy.

The initial disbelief gave way to an overwhelming sense of violation. Gisèle's mind reeled with questions. How had she been so blind to his duplicity? How could she have lived under the same roof with a man capable of such depravity? The weight of shame and guilt pressed heavily on her, even though she was not to blame.

In the days that followed, Gisèle wrestled with despair. She thought of ending her life, unable to reconcile her memories of a loving marriage with the dark truth revealed. But beneath the anguish stirred a spark of resolve. She would not allow shame to silence her. If Dominique had spent years orchestrating her suffering in secrecy, she would now bring his crimes into the light.

Chapter 4

The Gathering Storm

The public revelation of Dominique Pelicot's crimes sent shockwaves through the small town of Mazan and quickly rippled across France. Police investigations that had begun quietly now escalated as officers pieced together the extent of Dominique's network. They identified dozens of men who had responded to his invitations to assault his drugged wife. Many of these men, seemingly ordinary citizens, were arrested in waves, their identities concealed as authorities prepared for what would become one of the largest and most horrifying trials in recent history.

The evidence was overwhelming. Dominique had meticulously cataloged his crimes, storing videos, photographs, and online conversations in organized folders. Through this digital archive, investigators identified 72 perpetrators, though not all could be located. The initial shock of his betrayal was compounded by the sheer scale of complicity. Each arrest brought new revelations, and the public's horror grew.

The media descended upon Avignon, where the trial was set to take place. Headlines painted Dominique as a monstrous figure, but it was the revelation of his wife’s suffering that gripped the nation. Who was this woman, unknowingly at the center of such darkness?

For Gisèle, the growing media attention was both daunting and empowering. The public's outrage became a source of strength as she prepared to confront not only her husband but also the men who had participated in his scheme. The courtroom in Avignon would not only bear witness to justice but also to the awakening of a nation grappling with its culture of complicity and silence.

Chapter 5

Unveiling the Evidence

The courtroom in Avignon became the stage for one of the most harrowing trials in modern French history. For three months, the gallery sat in stunned silence as the prosecution laid bare the chilling details of Dominique Pelicot's crimes. Video evidence, photographs, and transcripts of online conversations were presented, leaving no room for doubt about the horrors Gisèle had endured.

Gisèle sat in the front row, her presence unwavering, as prosecutors recounted the unspeakable acts committed against her. The court watched grainy videos of

Dominique orchestrating and participating in the assaults, inviting strangers he met online into their marital home. Some of the men had traveled great distances to partake in what they chillingly referred to as "sessions."

The most damning evidence came from Dominique's meticulously maintained archives. Folders labeled "her rapists," "abuse," and "nights alone" provided a grotesque roadmap of his crimes. Investigators revealed how Dominique had used tranquilizers to incapacitate Gisèle, allowing himself and others to assault her while she was unconscious. The drugs caused the health issues that had baffled doctors for years—blackouts, weight loss, and hair thinning.

Defendants tried to mount defenses, some claiming ignorance of the non-consensual nature of the acts, others pointing fingers at Dominique as the mastermind. But the evidence was incontrovertible, and the courtroom heard, over and over, the phrase: "Guilty of aggravated rape."

Through it all, Gisèle listened stoically. Her decision to face her abusers in open court became a testament to her resilience and a rallying cry for survivors everywhere.

Chapter 6

A Feminist Hero Emerges

As the trial progressed, Gisèle Pelicot's presence in the courtroom took on symbolic significance. By waiving her right to anonymity, she transformed from a private victim into a public figure of resilience and defiance. Each day, she walked into the courthouse, facing her abusers and the weight of the evidence with remarkable composure. Her quiet dignity stood in stark contrast to the depravity of the crimes being revealed.

Outside the courthouse, a movement was growing. Feminist activists, survivors of sexual violence, and supporters from across France rallied behind Gisèle. Signs reading "Merci, Gisèle" and "A rape is a rape" were held aloft by crowds that gathered daily. Social media buzzed with hashtags celebrating her courage, and her image—once known only to her family and neighbors—became a symbol of strength and justice.

Gisèle's decision to go public was a turning point. She articulated her reasons with profound clarity: "Shame must change sides. It belongs to the perpetrators, not the victims." Her words resonated deeply, igniting discussions about consent, rape culture, and the systemic failures that allowed her suffering to persist for years.

Her courage reverberated far beyond the walls of the courtroom. Women across France began sharing their own stories, inspired by Gisèle's bravery. Men, too, were prompted to examine their complicity in perpetuating a culture of silence. As the trial unfolded, Gisèle became more than a survivor; she became a feminist hero, galvanizing a nation to confront its darkest truths.

Chapter 7

The Verdict

The air in the Avignon courthouse was electric with anticipation as the trial reached its climax. On the final day of proceedings, supporters gathered outside, their chants echoing through the stone corridors. Inside, Gisèle Pelicot sat with her children by her side, her expression resolute. The presiding judge, Roger Arata, prepared to deliver the verdicts in what had become one of the most significant trials in French legal history.

One by one, the names of Dominique Pelicot and the 50 co-defendants were read aloud, each accompanied by the grim announcement: "Guilty of aggravated rape." The majority of the accused received sentences ranging from 8 to 10 years, while Dominique, the orchestrator of the abuse, was handed the maximum penalty of 20 years. Though many considered this lenient given the gravity of the crimes, it marked a decisive moment of justice for Gisèle.

The courtroom was silent as the judge detailed the profound betrayal Dominique had committed against his wife of five decades. Gisèle's courage in waiving her anonymity and enduring the grueling trial was praised, with Arata calling her a symbol of strength in the fight against sexual violence.

Outside, the crowd erupted in cheers as the news spread. Signs reading “Merci Gisèle” waved in the air, and chants of support filled the streets. For Gisèle, the verdict was bittersweet—a measure of justice for her, but also a painful reminder of what she had endured. Still, she hoped it would serve as a warning: silence and complicity must no longer shield abusers.

Chapter 8

Monsieur Tout-le-Monde

The profiles of the perpetrators in Gisèle's story reflect a shocking ordinariness, which speaks volumes about the insidious nature of systemic misogyny and rape culture. These men, seemingly harmless and unremarkable—often described as "Monsieur Tout-le-Monde," or "everyman"—represent the normalization of violence against women in society. Their ordinariness emphasizes that the culture of abuse is not perpetrated by a few outliers, but by individuals who blend into daily life, who could be anyone. This makes the issue even more dangerous, as it suggests that rape and harassment are not isolated incidents but rather embedded in the fabric of societal norms.

The fact that these perpetrators often present themselves as regular family men or successful professionals reveals how rape culture thrives in plain sight. The invisibility of their crimes until revealed forces society to confront its deeply ingrained gender inequalities. It becomes evident that their actions are not merely personal failures, but the result of a larger cultural failure to challenge patriarchal systems. These perpetrators are not monsters, but ordinary individuals whose privilege, entitlement, and refusal to acknowledge women's autonomy perpetuate a cycle of abuse. This chapter exposes how everyday interactions, whether in the workplace, in relationships, or even within families, are often tinged with subtle misogyny, making it all the more difficult to recognize and address sexual violence.

Chapter 9

The National Debate

The aftermath of Gisèle's case catalyzed a national debate that brought issues of consent, legal reforms, and societal attitudes to the forefront. Public discussions began to shift towards the recognition of sexual violence not as isolated acts but as part of a larger cultural pattern that needed to be addressed. The conversations surrounding consent evolved significantly, with a growing awareness of the importance of clear, mutual agreement in any sexual encounter. This recognition led to calls for legal reforms, particularly in how cases of sexual violence are prosecuted, and how survivors are treated by the justice system.

Feminist movements, both local and global, seized this moment to demand better protections for women and a cultural reckoning with the entrenched sexism in legal and social structures. These movements called for stronger laws, more comprehensive support systems for survivors, and public education on the dynamics of abuse and consent. As the debates continued, a cultural shift began to take shape. The #MeToo movement, already gaining momentum globally, found new energy in Gisèle's story, and more women began to feel empowered to speak out against their own experiences. This chapter explores the ways in which society began to question its longstanding attitudes toward gender, power, and sexuality.

Chapter 10

Facing the Past

In this chapter, Gisèle reflects on her life with Dominique, examining the complex psychological and cultural factors that enabled her abuse to persist undetected for so long. Gisèle's childhood plays a crucial role in her understanding of the circumstances that allowed Dominique's abuse to continue unchecked. Growing up in a society that often downplays the seriousness of emotional and physical abuse, she internalized harmful beliefs about her own worth and the role of women in relationships. The normalization of patriarchal values within her family and community made it difficult to recognize the signs of abuse or to question the dynamics of power that Dominique exerted over her.

As Gisèle confronts her past, she comes to realize the profound impact that a culture of silence and shame has had on her ability to speak out. She reflects on how deeply embedded cultural narratives about female subjugation and male entitlement shaped her understanding of relationships, making it harder for her to identify the abuse as it was happening. This chapter delves into the intricate process of self-examination, as Gisèle works to untangle the psychological scars of her past and understand how society's cultural and institutional forces allowed her suffering to remain hidden. Her journey of reflection becomes a crucial part of her healing, as she acknowledges the deep societal factors that allowed the abuse to flourish in the first place.

Chapter 11

Building Strength

Gisèle's journey to reclaim her life is one of resilience and determination. In this chapter, we follow her healing process, which includes therapy, activism, and finding solidarity with other survivors. Therapy becomes a crucial tool for Gisèle to confront the trauma she endured and rebuild her sense of self. Through counseling, she gains the strength to process her past, understand the effects of her abuse, and develop healthy coping mechanisms. Therapy also offers a space for Gisèle to understand her own worth and her right to be treated with respect and dignity.

Alongside therapy, Gisèle turns to activism as a way of reclaiming her power. She becomes a voice for other survivors, advocating for legal reforms and greater societal awareness of the issues of sexual violence and systemic abuse. Through her activism, Gisèle finds solidarity with other survivors who share her pain and strength, creating a community of support that helps her continue her healing journey. This chapter highlights the importance of community and activism in the recovery process, as Gisèle's work empowers not only herself but others to reclaim their voices and demand change.

Chapter 12

The Feminist Wave

The impact of Gisèle's courage reverberates far beyond her own life. Her story becomes a catalyst for a broader feminist wave that gains momentum across the country. Grassroots movements, fueled by Gisèle's bravery, begin to challenge not just the legal system but also the cultural attitudes that perpetuate sexual violence. These movements are joined by male allies who confront their own complicity in a culture that has too often excused or ignored abuse. Men, too, begin to examine their roles in perpetuating patriarchal norms and engage in conversations about accountability, empathy, and respect.

As the feminist movement gains traction, legislative changes follow. The legal system begins to reform, with stricter laws around consent and greater protection for survivors of sexual violence. The government responds with new initiatives aimed at raising awareness, providing resources for survivors, and ensuring that perpetrators are held accountable. This chapter explores how Gisèle's personal journey sparked a cultural shift that empowered both women and men to confront sexual violence head-on and work toward a society that prioritizes safety, respect, and equality.

Chapter 13

Merci Gisèle

In the final chapter, the nation expresses its gratitude to Gisèle. The "Merci Gisèle" banners and chants become powerful symbols of a society that acknowledges the courage of survivors and the profound impact they have had on the collective consciousness. Gisèle's story is no longer just hers; it is the story of every survivor who has fought for justice and healing. Her actions have inspired a new generation of activists, and her legacy is one of change, empowerment, and hope.

As Gisèle reflects on her journey, she expresses her hopes for future generations. She envisions a world where sexual violence is no longer tolerated, where survivors are believed and supported, and where consent is a fundamental principle in every interaction. Gisèle's journey is a testament to the power of one individual to spark societal change, and the "Merci Gisèle" movement represents the collective acknowledgment of the work still to be done. This final chapter captures the profound gratitude of a nation, while also emphasizing the ongoing struggle for justice and equality that continues beyond Gisèle's personal journey.

Conclusion

The case involving Gisèle Pelicot, her ex-husband Dominique Pelicot, and the 50 other men who participated in her abuse has left an indelible mark on France, sparking nationwide conversations about sexual violence, consent, and rape culture. Gisèle Pelicot's incredible courage in making her trauma public has transformed her into a feminist icon and sparked important dialogues about how society views sexual violence.

Dominique Pelicot's horrific actions, which spanned nearly a decade, were enabled by his systematic abuse of his wife, drugging her to render her unconscious while inviting other men to assault her. His conviction, along with the sentencing of 50 other men, has sent a strong message about the need to address the systemic nature of such abuses and the complicity of those involved. Gisèle's decision to waive her right to anonymity and publicly confront her abusers has not only empowered her but also inspired countless others to speak out about their own experiences with violence.

The case also highlighted significant flaws in legal frameworks, including the question of consent and the need to revise legal definitions to include explicit acknowledgment of non-consensual acts. It challenged entrenched attitudes toward sexual violence and the perpetrators of such crimes, showing that those who participate in these acts are often ordinary individuals who live among us.

Moreover, the trial has sparked a broader cultural reckoning with toxic masculinity, the normalization of sexual violence, and the complicity of bystanders. The public's reaction, particularly in the form of rallies and demonstrations of support for Gisèle, demonstrates a shift in how society views sexual violence. This case serves as a pivotal moment in the ongoing struggle for justice, equality, and the protection of women's rights, marking a potential turning point in how sexual abuse is perceived and addressed.

Made in the USA
Coppell, TX
05 May 2025

49019161R00026